P9-AZV-683

Pig Pig Returns

David McPhail

Charlesbridge

For Yolanda. Hey, it was her idea.

A note for concerned readers: Pig Pig is of the appropriate age, height, and weight to be sitting in the front seat of an automobile. On pages 8 and 9 his safety belt is obscured by his magazine and the dashboard of the car.

Published by Charlesbridge
85 Main Street
Watertown, MA 02472
(617) 926-0329
www.charlesbridge.com

Library of Congress Cataloging-in-Publication Data
McPhail, David, 1940–
Pig Pig returns / David McPhail.
p. cm.
Summary: Pig Pig is concerned about traveling across the country with his aunt and uncle, but is even more worried when he returns.
ISBN 978-1-58089-356-5 (reinforced for library use)
[1. Automobile travel—Fiction. 2. Aunts—Fiction. 3. Uncles—Fiction. 4. Vacations—Fiction. 5. Pigs—Fiction.] I. Title.
PZ7.M2427Pj 2011
[E]—dc22 2010023528

Printed in China
(hc) 10 9 8 7 6 5 4 3 2 1

Illustrations done in pen and ink and watercolor on Arches paper
Display type and text type set in Goudy
Color separations by Chroma Graphics, Singapore
Printed and bound February 2011 by Yangjiang Millenium Litho Ltd. in Yangjiang, Guangdong, China
Production supervision by Brian G. Walker
Designed by Susan Mallory Sherman

Pig Pig didn't want to spend summer vacation traveling across the country with Aunt Wilma and Uncle Fred.

He just wanted to stay home with his mother and his cat, Fluffy.

There were so many things he wanted to do. He had a new rocket ship model to assemble, and who would do his chores while he was gone?

But mostly Pig Pig was concerned that his mother and Fluffy would miss him too much.

Don't worry, dear.... I'll feed Fluffy and put out the trash.

But his aunt and uncle were so insistent.

So he went.

Uncle Fred urged Pig Pig to take in the sights of the open road, but Pig Pig insisted on catching up on back issues of his favorite magazine, *Daring Pig Exploits*.

Daring Pig

An emergency stop was soon required.

Back on the road, Pig Pig decided to look out the window. The tired old car chugged to the top of Buzzard Mountain for the spectacular view . . .

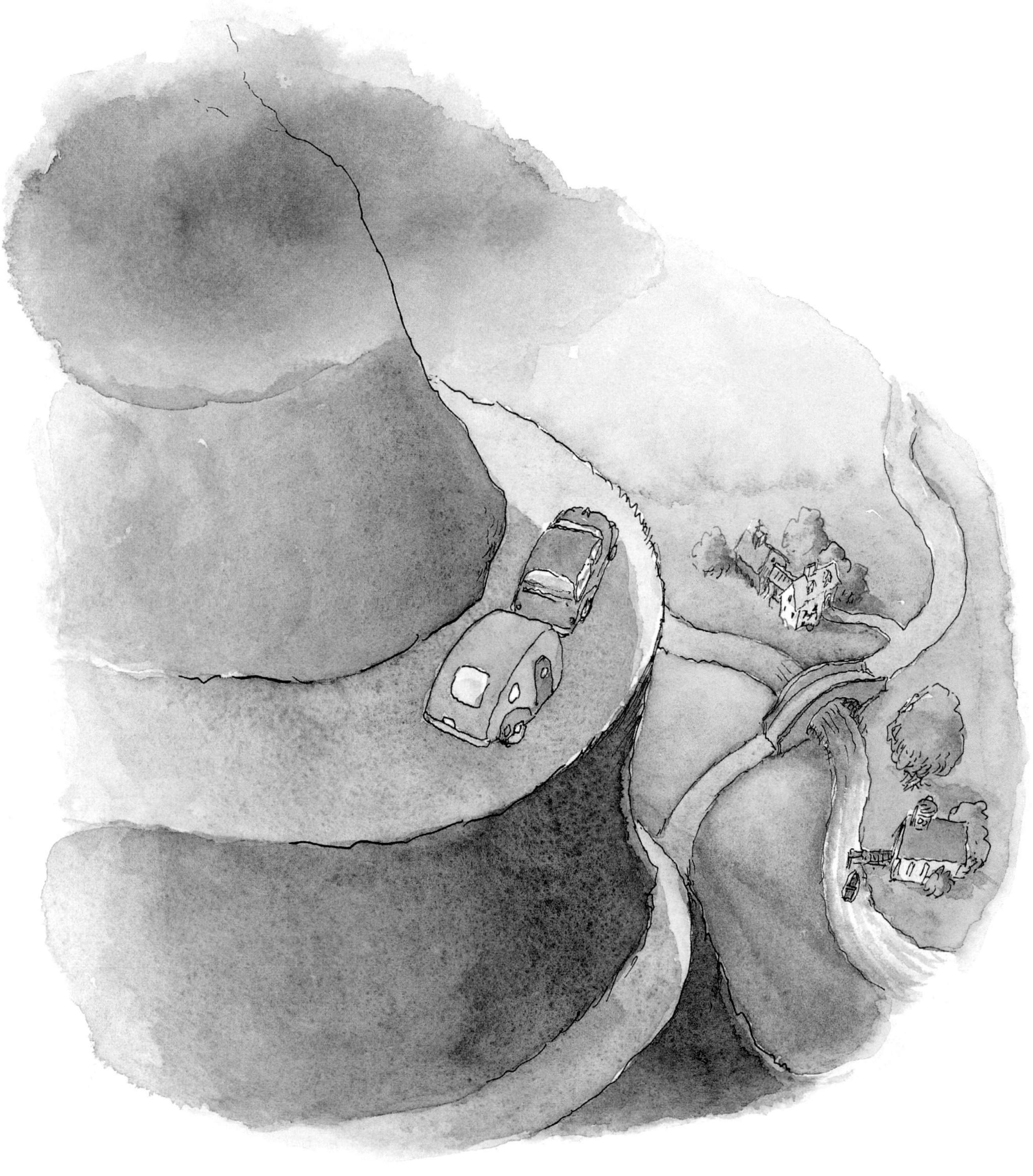

but when they got there, it was a little cloudy.

Next was the hot springs where water squirted fifty feet into the air every Thursday afternoon. Unfortunately they arrived there on a Friday.

SNACKS
CLOSED

Then they visited the world's biggest ball of yarn.

They saw a house made entirely from soda cans. Pig Pig found it interesting and wrote about it in a postcard to his mother.

Then he had his picture taken on a boulder
that looked like an elephant. That was exciting!

Say "Cheese."

They peered into a deep hole that the guide said went all the way to China. Pig Pig was suitably impressed.

And how could he ever forget the famous three-legged chicken?

Pig Pig was having a great vacation with Aunt Wilma and Uncle Fred. He couldn't believe he hadn't wanted to come.

All too soon it was time to go home.

He sent his mother a postcard saying he would be there soon.

Pig Pig was excited, but he was also worried. What if Fluffy didn't remember him?

What if his mother had rented his room to a stranger? Or had given all his toys away? What if she'd forgotten how he liked his oatmeal?

Or had canceled his subscription to *Daring Pig Exploits*?

Poor Pig Pig.

His fears only got worse when Aunt Wilma stopped the camper in front of Pig Pig's house. No one was there to greet him. Had his mother forgotten him?

Had she and Fluffy moved away?

But just when he thought he might start bawling, he caught a whiff of something good—the smell of oatmeal cooking!

Pig Pig leaped from the car and dashed up the walk. Just as he did, the front door flew open and there was his mother . . . with Fluffy beside her!

Pig Pig ran into his mother's waiting arms, and after a long, big hug, he bent down and picked up Fluffy, who licked Pig Pig on the snout.

WELCOM

Then Pig Pig, Aunt Wilma, and Uncle Fred went inside to share stories of their adventures over warm bowls of oatmeal.

Pig Pig had had a wonderful time . . .

but he was happy to be home.